CALL ME
ESTEBAN

DESIGN & LAYOUT Nikša Eršek
PUBLISHED BY Sandorf Passage
South Portland, Maine, United States
sandorfpassage.org
IMPRINT OF Sandorf
Severinska 30, Zagreb, Croatia
PRINTED BY Znanje, Zagreb
Originally published by Dobra knjiga as *Zovite me Esteban*.
Cover Photograph © Ivana Nobilo

Sandorf Passage books are available to the
trade through Independent Publishers Group:
ipgbook.com | (800) 888-4741.

National and University Library Zagreb
Control Number: 001100732

Library of Congress Control Number:
2021936943

ISBN: 978-9-53351-324-9

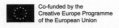

Co-funded by the
Creative Europe Programme
of the European Union

The European Commission support for the
production of this publication does not constitute
an endorsement of the contents which reflects the
views only of the authors, and the Commission
cannot be held responsible for any use which may
be made of the information contained therein.

This Book is published with financial support by
the Republic of Croatia's Ministry of Culture and Media.

LEJLA KALAMUJIĆ

CALL ME ESTEBAN

TRANSLATED BY JENNIFER ZOBLE

SAN–
DORF
PAS–
SAGE

SOUTH PORTLAND | MAINE

Note on the pronunciation of names

We have maintained the original spelling of proper nouns. The vowels are pronounced as in Italian. The consonants are pronounced as follows:

c = ts, as in *bits*
č = ch
ć = similar to č, like the t in *future*
dž = g, as in *general*
đ = similar to dž
j = y, as in *yellow*
r = trilled as in Scottish; sometimes used as a vowel, e.g. "Krk," roughly "Kirk"
š = sh
ž = like the s in *pleasure*

Contents

What's a Typewriter to Me?

RAINY MORNING, NOWHERE to go. I sit on the loveseat and leaf through the newspaper. Kiki curls up at my feet, purring. On page 28, the emboldened headline:

LAST TYPEWRITER FACTORY IN THE WORLD CLOSES ITS DOORS
It's Tuesday, April 26, 2011. I read further:

The era of the typewriter, the 20th-century mainstay of office equipment, has come to an end. In Mumbai, India, the last factory to produce typewriters has suspended operations.

My mother was a typist. During a time that they say no longer matters. During a short life that lasted only twenty-two years. She died on a Friday long ago, August 20, 1982. I was two years old.

My life contains no memories of my mother. She's only a story, a sacred one, of origins, of intimate prehistories. My peers fell asleep to fairy tales; I listened to tales about her. Her death was spoken about quietly. The murmur would be turned up only with the occasional anecdote or escapade from her life. Then the lost time inflamed the vocal cords. It rolled between the tongue and palate; it formed words, then sentences, from air. The stories traced her journey. It didn't matter that sometimes one story negated another, that contradictions arose: one doesn't question the sacred, one can only believe in it.

It was the time of the youth work actions, when everyone would return home with kidney trouble. It was the world where typing competitions were held and awards were given for second place. Second place because some girl cried when my mother was faster and better. As a consolation the jury gave the crying girl the trophy and sent my mother home with a second-place certificate. Aside from that certificate, all that remains from her are her bathrobe, her wedding ring, her Communist Party membership card, and her typewriter.

In my grandparents' apartment the typewriter was a relic. A carefully preserved memory in the bedroom closet. Only my relentless appeals could coax it to the table. Grandma and Grandpa would sit next to me and let me type. Sharp sounds ricocheted off the walls. Ink impressed the shapes of randomly selected letters onto the white paper. And then words, sentences... All the way till the end of the line, when the lever sent the cylinder back to the beginning. I'd type like this for an hour or two. When my fingers finally hurt, we'd wrap the typewriter in its plastic bag, in the deep silence of untimely death.

Was it then that I fell in love with writing? I don't know. But I know that I loved to type up the short scenes and episodes from her life. When she broke the window in the living room and made like nothing had happened. Or even better, when she ate the whole ham but regarded the empty plate in my grandmother's hands with great surprise, repeating, "Where did it go?"

I don't know why the news from India bothered me. Nor do I know why I climbed the ladder and retrieved the dusty case from the top of the closet. I can't remember the last time I touched it. Soon it will be thirty years since my mother died.

LEJLA KALAMUJIĆ

I contemplate this while inserting an empty sheet of paper and typing:

What's a typewriter to me?

The Four Seasons

THEIR VOICES SPEAK through their eyes. Young and old. Tender, pleasant. I could spread them on my body, like butter on a hot roll. With hot cheeks, I would lick their questions from open palms:

Who are you? Whose are you?

I, the golden one (as I was nicknamed), belonged to summer. In summer I was born. In summer my mother died. In that summer of life and death we were together: Grandma Brana, Grandpa Boro, Nana Safeta, Papa Nedžad, and me. Dad both was and wasn't there. As one family, one house, in two places, in two different parts of town, we ate Nana's pita and Grandma's sarma, and both of my grandfathers drank beer and rakija. Our tenants were God and Tito.

I am of the summer! Summer, that's me.

The voices laughed. Thick fingers pinched my cheeks until they turned red as copper. The tenants would appear here and there. First in Nana and Papa's prayers, and then in Grandma and Grandpa's Partisan songs.

And then the shooting began.

One half of the house—Grandma Brana, Grandpa Boro, and I—went to Grandma's sister's place in Šid. This was my first betrayal. I went with Grandma and Grandpa, leaving Nana and Papa behind. In this half of the house, which never stood firmly on the ground, we got a new tenant: War. He showed up continually: when we'd be eating, bathing, dealing with diarrhea or constipation. We also had waves. But not sea waves, not the kind that pull fish, shells, barges. These waves lived at the home of one Sreten. He was an older gentleman with a massive ham radio. We would go to his place on Saturdays, in sun, rain, and snow. Sreten would start up the radio, offering us homemade elderflower juice and three stools. We'd sit there and release our voices, rather than our bodies, to the waves. On good days we'd encounter the voices of Nana Safeta and Papa Nedžad; they'd tell us they were still alive and that this shit would blow over soon. I came to hate this half of the house, and our tenant. I imagined pulling his hair, poking him in the eyes, pouring salt in his nostrils. But I didn't dare. He was too big and strong.

And then the shooting briefly stopped.

I left that half, and Grandma Brana and Grandpa Boro in it, and headed back to the other half of the house, where Nana Safeta and Papa Nedžad were. That was my second betrayal. In this half, things were bad. The truce lasted only a short time. Then shooting again. We didn't have windows, only thick nylon sheets, and a stove called a sanduklija that merely farted rather than warming us. I would sit in my tiny room and write letters to Grandma Brana and Grandpa Boro on Red Cross message forms. And here too we had a tenant, and he too was called War. I didn't know him well. I didn't dare touch him. I just hid his socks and pants, and sometimes I would spit in his powdered eggs, in hopes he'd get the message and leave on his own.

And then autumn came.

Grenades falling. Nana Safeta and I sit by the farting stove. I cry. The waves bring a voice that says Grandpa Boro has died.

In his sleep. A tear falling from his eye. Nana Safeta sighs, which unnerves me deeply. Papa Nedžad enters, with a shy smile on his face and a copy of *Oslobođenje* in his hand. He sits beside the two of us and triumphantly turns the newspaper's pages till just before the end. A short obituary, among many, of Grandpa Boro, and a picture of him.

Papa Nedžad says, "Never mind the shooting, I went out last night and got it in the paper, so everyone would know."

Yes, Boro had died, somewhere far from the war—so it was whispered later around our half of the house. Yes, I say, Boro died, with a tear on his cheek, and I'd bet my life that he died thinking I didn't love him anymore, because I'd left. My betrayal deepened.

And then spring came.

In our half of the house it was Nana Safeta, Papa Nedžad, and me. War had moved out, supposedly. A year before. But what a mess he left behind. You've never seen such a pig. We waited for Peace to move into our spare room. He was meant to come, but somehow didn't. And we were counting on that rent. We needed it to live. I'd enrolled in high school. Life costs money. No sign of Peace, and Nana fell ill. The doctors said it was brain cancer, and gave her a month or two, at most. Everything was drifting away from me, as on a vast open sea. Now I hated this half of the house. I slept a lot.

One morning Nana Safeta, too weak to stand, calls out my name and asks me to come help her. I'm not quite awake: I hear her, yet I don't hear her. Somehow I manage to rouse myself and stumble to her bed. She offers me her hand, like the feeble branch of an ancient tree. I tug and tug, but nothing. She's heavy, too heavy. I tug a little more, then stop. I say: "I can't." I go back to bed. I fall asleep instantly. Nana Safeta died the next day. I became an even bigger traitor.

And then winter happened.

Ah, yes. I've almost forgotten to say that Peace had finally moved into our half of the house. That fraud. Totally friendly, full of words and smiles. And never a pfennig of rent. Always tomorrow, the day after tomorrow, just one more day. A real sleazebag. Papa Nedžad communicated with him; I avoided them both. Nedžad wanted us to talk. He even gave me permission to smoke in his presence when we drank coffee, as long as we were together. But I couldn't be bothered. They got on my nerves: him, the house, and Peace. I'd begun studying philosophy at the university; that winter I listened to lectures on German classical idealism. I made fantastic charts summarizing the ideas of each philosopher. When I'd go for coffee with my friends, I'd carefully arrange my charts at the table, so we could trace each phase of being. At that time Grandma Brana moved her half of the house to Bijeljina. I guess some kind of Peace had come to her as well. But he was the same delinquent. She wrote me, called me. I didn't reciprocate. Those fucking phases of being, with no free time. Grandma grew more ill. She was alone. One day the news came that she'd died.

We go to the funeral, Papa Nedžad and I. I'm so pissed off I don't say a word. We walk to the grave. I'm first in line, immediately behind the casket. The procession is slow. I recall Sofka Nikolić, the superstar singer in the Kingdom of Yugoslavia. Sofka had a daughter, Marica, who contracted tuberculosis at an early age, poor thing. Sofka was never at her side: London, Paris, Vienna. The queen of the bohemian quarter, Skadarlija, garnered fame on all the world's stages. Marica died. At seventeen. The story goes that this killed Sofka. She came here to Bijeljina, to bury Marica, to build her a big crypt. And she bought a house right by the cemetery, to be near her. She lived there for years, until she herself died. Now both of them are in the crypt, one beside the other.

As I walk behind my grandmother's casket, I think about Sofka, and Marica, and everything else irks me, the crying people, and the sky, and the earth. I behave rudely. The cemetery workers lower Grandma Brana into the burial plot. An unpleasant silence. Everyone stares at me. Since I was the only person she had left, I'm supposed to be the first one to toss a clump of earth into her grave. Someone whispers to me that, if I really can't, I can throw a flower instead. The grave is deep, cold, Decembrous. My mother, Brana's daughter, died in summer. A summer long ago, in another city. I peer into the grave that's claiming that half of the house and think about how stupid everyone is. Unforgivably stupid. What does it matter what falls first onto a casket of carved and sanded oak? Now, when it's clear that Brana will not lie in the ground next to her daughter, who, I should add, was named after snow: Snežana.

Between one summer and one fall came Papa Nedžad's turn. But he was really off his rocker, causing chaos all over the hospital. In the middle of the night he tore out his roommate's catheter, assuring the man that he didn't need it. He was senile; people in the hallway would beg me to take him home. To our half of the house, I mean. At the end the nurses had to strap him to his bed. With virtually no consciousness left, he thanked them profusely, then turned to me: "Bring me some scissors." For two days he continued to breathe, but I knew he wasn't there anymore. This time I witnessed it, which perhaps lessened my betrayal just a bit. I gazed at the tubes stuck in his emaciated body. Like roots that siphoned life irrevocably into the underground waters of death. I sat at his bedside while people passed by the room. At some point a doctor came and took his pulse, checked his tubes and monitor. Then she turned to me: "It won't be much longer, an hour or two."

That evening, on my way home from the hospital, I stopped at a bench in Veliki Park to smoke a cigarette. I wasn't angry. It had been quite some time since I'd hated the people around me; now I just hated myself. I watched the others while they moved through their lives. They regarded me casually. I heard their voices inside me.

Who are you?

Whose are you?

Betrayal is a dangerous condition. Hard to cure. I know this today, after years of more or less unsuccessful therapy. Today, summer is mine. And autumn is mine. God and Tito are mine. War is mine. And Peace. And winter and spring are mine. Everything is mine. Now that I have nothing left.

Waiting for the Pigeons

DAD LOVED PIGEONS. After Mom's death, the two of us returned to the family house in Vratnik, where we lived with Nana and Papa. And the pigeons. And a few cats that lurked in the garden at night, curled up and treacherously purring beneath the pigeon coop. Papa wasn't too keen on that arrangement: feathers, crumbs, stench everywhere. But life needed to be built anew, cobbled together like that coop of old wire and board.

Papa would work every day in the garage. Sweaty, his plump belly protruding from under his tight T-shirt. He'd spend hours sawing, sanding, hammering. He mounted the coop high on the wall facing the garden. We had tall ladders I was forbidden to climb. "You'll fall and hurt yourself!" Nana would reply at my pleading.

That's why climbing was my secret adventure. I'd sneak up the ladder, stepping carefully so the rungs didn't creak. And the cats? They'd dart around and leap at the wall. Their claws would softly scrape its rough surface. Then they'd tumble down, howling. Only the nimblest prevailed in this nighttime ascent. The odd pigeon suffered: in the morning Dad would find it bloodied, its throat slashed. But Death, that fiend, they concealed from me like snake feet. They buried the dead pigeons in the garden and covered the freshly dug earth with leaves.

At dawn, Dad fed the pigeons assorted seed. He poured them fresh water, they drank, and then, their beaks still wet, they took flight among the clouds. Everyone headed off at the same time: the pigeons to freedom, and Dad to the post office, where he worked. I was awakened by Nana's voice and the scent of breakfast. Nana eternally on her feet, music gurgling from the ancient radio. Nana would break into song; she said it helped her work. While she stirred the makings of lunch on the stove, scrubbed the sink, or dusted the bedside tables, the songs tumbled forth—thus was Nana able to blend the life of a homemaker and the dreams of a chanteuse.

I eat breakfast in my pajamas. My eyes sting from the crusty sleep. I head back to my room with two slices of buttered toast on a copper plate. I sit on my bed, legs tucked under the quilt, and set the plate in front of me, taking a big bite of toast. I chew slowly and gaze out the window. When I'm finished eating, I dress in front of the mirror. Tucked in its corner is a photo of my father, in a blue work uniform, smiling. He holds a pair of pliers and a spool of wire. Dad sets up telephone lines for the postal service, connects voices. Like the pigeons connecting heaven and earth in their flight. I pull on my socks as I run out of the house. In the garden, the huge stone table is waiting for me. I lie atop it, spreading my wings and scanning the sky for pigeons. The high-flying ones perforate the clouds; the looping, turning ones whirl to unconsciousness. The hours pass. My eyes are tethered to the sky. To that high, high place where, I'm told, live only those who are no more.

Panic descends when a hawk appears. I leap to my feet, wave my arms, shout and hiss, but my voice can't reach those heights. I race to get Nana and Papa. "A hawk is gonna eat the pigeons!" I

LEJLA KALAMUJIĆ

cry. Papa hurries from the garage; Nana rushes down the stairs. They smack their hands together. Nana yells "Pis!" at the hawk. When the aerial chase ends, luckily for the pigeons, Papa curses the birds, the plumage, the pigeon poop. Then he asks Nana what time it is. As he makes for the garage, she calls out, "He's on his way now, you'll see."

I go in when the sun streaks westward. The smell of food is dissipating. The radio is silent. The wall clock ticks as shadows slip through the windows. I part the curtains and peek out at the pigeon coop. Only Miki is there. He's a rock pigeon. An excellent flier! When he walks, he waddles a little. Like the way Dad sways when he comes home at night.

"Look at the time, and no sight of him," begins Papa.

"He's coming now."

"You said that three hours ago."

"Maybe he got held up at work."

"He's at the bar, I know it. Every night the same thing."

And the silence has its own voice.

"He better not think he's getting in here tonight."

"Oh, stop it," says Nana.

The shadows lengthen. Like a cat, I creep out of the house with them. The door to the pigeon coop is still open. Step by step, I make my way up the ladder. One rung, two, three . . . It's quiet at the top. And I can see better. I perch there and wait for the pigeons to return.

In Vain You Wake Her

Surely she said: let him search for me and see I'm gone
that woman with a child's hands whom I love
that child who fell asleep not wiping her tears whom I wake
in vain in vain in vain
in vain I wake her

BRANKO MILJKOVIĆ, "Uzalud je budim"
(In Vain I Wake Her)

I LIE IN BED, pressing my eyelids together, my lashes itching. I pretend to sleep. I pretend I won't hear the commotion in the kitchen that's about to begin. I know it will. Papa will throw a fit when he comes home drunk; Nana will cry; Auntie will retreat into her own world. Inside my eyes there's just darkness, like a deep, scabrous sky in which desires dry up, unfulfilled. The uproar arrives! Then it's over. Passed. Anger cascades into footfalls. The old floorboards of the house in Vratnik creak wildly. Then silence comes, and with it a pair of steps: they linger awkwardly at the door to my room. Come on, come in, I think, my eyes squeezed shut.

We lie on our backs. The pillows cushion our bent arms, large and small. Our heads rest on them. You wake her. You speak slowly of her, your dead wife, your beautiful wife. Every once in a while, it occurs to you that I don't remember her, so you explain, in depth. As always, you pull skirt after skirt from the closet where her things are stored. The navy one, the white one, the olive one. You take them with fingertips that grasp the edge of the fabric like clothespins, you spread them out and gather them together, you inspect them, you inevitably stroke them with your right palm to remove any dust. I know they'll never fit me, I don't say.

And you keep talking about her. About your dead wife, your beautiful wife. It's late. Your voice grows silent. The words dissolve on your tongue. You falter, lose yourself. You're a child who falls asleep not wiping his tears. I watch you while you sleep, unaware that I'll hate you one day. Not because of you, that's not it. You were just a brat, sniveling, lost. I will hate you because of all the people who howl at you. The ones who swear at you in the street while you wake her. I will hate you because of the kids' clumsy sidelong looks, their nudging and pinching, their barely audible snickering when we play marbles, when your swaying body appears at the end of the street.

Alcohol molecules fill the room like water flooding the shore at high tide. The name of my mother reeks of alcohol. I breathe it in evenly, gazing at the ceiling. The pigeons sleep in their cage.

We'll demolish the room in a few years. We'll peel off the wallpaper ourselves, hire a housepainter to scrape the walls bare. I'll clean zealously, cramming a 30-liter bin with the refuse and barely managing to haul it to the dumpster. Trudging down the street, I'll smell the scent of your tears for the last time. Dragging myself to the trash heap, I'll see us once again lying with our arms flung across the pillows. I watch the ceiling, and you wake her tearfully. Her, your dead wife, your beautiful wife. But by then I'll already know: I hate you.

I hate you because the sky is deep and scabrous, and there is nothing you can do about it.

White Desert

THE FIRST WINTER of the war, in exile. Grandma, Grandpa, and me, in a small village with a short name on the border of Vojvodina. It's a school holiday, and I beg my great uncle to take me along to his bakery. He starts his yellow van and leaves it running for a few minutes to warm up. While he opens the gate, I quickly put on my coat and boots. I grab the bag containing the salad, pies, and sausages Grandma and Auntie have prepared for us to eat with the flat, round bread known as lepinje. Bakery work is nocturnal. We head out before it gets dark. The sky is white, but there's no snow yet. Cold wind whips around the empty terraces, as if through hollow bones. People scurry, mice-like, to their warm abodes, chimneys puffing smoke. Šid, winter of '93. I'm far from home.

In the bakery, the lit oven awaits us. My subzero skin begins to thaw. I pull off my boots and remove my coat and hat, replacing them with a white apron and small cap. I become a baker. The old master Uncle Franjo has prepared everything. The first batch of dough is rising in the electric mixer, like the Miljacka River during a heavy rain. The other employees trickle in. They blow hot breath into their blue hands. "Still no snow," they say.

The hours pass slowly. I get underfoot, doing what's needed and not needed. Uncle lets me do everything. I weigh the dough for the lepinje. When I stand on an upturned plastic crate, I can reach the counter where the dough is taking shape. I grab a piece and form it into a stick figure. I tell everyone that it's meant to be me. In Sarajevo I used to be good at soccer; in hopes of achieving athletic glory I even chose a new name for myself: Lejlan. The employees laugh. I prattle on about Sarajevo, about my pals down the street. The stick figure, or rather, the mini-stick, is ready for baking.

The timer goes off. The bread's now ready to come out of the oven. I pull on thick gloves, a few sizes too large, and retrieve loaf after loaf, my palms growing sweaty. Using a brush, I scrape the charred edges of crust from the bottom of each loaf. I take the stick figure, and carefully brush and blow on it, like God creating Adam and Eve. Bits of singed flour fly from its baked body. I don't put the stick figure in the basket with the rest of the bread. I set it aside, for myself, for later.

Around three in the morning is the most critical time. But tonight, I can't resist sleeping. One hour will be enough. I amble to the stockroom and lie down on a big bag of flour. And miss the snow's arrival.

I stay there until 4:30 or so. Everyone is in high spirits, as if the night has just begun: they're looking forward to being in the snow. It fell unbelievably fast, they say, turning everything white. I sit on the plastic crate and eat the stick figure. I tear off a piece, chew it methodically, swallow. The head disappears, then the hands, then the body, all of it.

Young people bring in the snow. They stop at the bakery for warm lepinje on their way home from the bars. Their hair is white, along with the tops of their shoulders and shoes. The local representatives of political parties come in for hundreds

LEJLA KALAMUJIĆ

of loaves, to take to rallies in Belgrade. At 5:30 we throw in the last batch. Uncle tells me to get ready to leave, to go home and sleep, there's no need to wait for him. Our house isn't far from the bakery—just three blocks.

My first wartime snowfall far from home. I don't feel like sleeping. Every once in a while, I pause to write my name in the snow with my finger. I remember how Grandma told me she'd named my mother Snežana because of the snijeg, the snow that fell on the night of her birth. And Mama, Sneška, lived here the first year of her life. Grandma still cherishes a photograph from that time. Sneška, small and grubby, in suspendered pants and slushy rubber boots, looking more like a Sneško, a snowman, than a Sneška.

At that first snowy daybreak, in the winter of '93, I decide to make my own Sneško. I gather snow and pack it together like flour, but it slips from my gloves. I take them off and try again with my bare hands. The dry snow, more like gunpowder than flour, won't bind. I try another time, and another, who knows how many. The wind blows the white flakes in all directions. They whirl through the air, covering the roofs and the benches along the main street, stealing onto the verandas. Everything becomes white. Including me. My eyes sting. I blink. The wind is all-powerful; it won't let me walk. I crouch in the middle of the whiteness, wind howling around me, wildly, reproachfully. I sit there, without Sneško, without Sneška, without anything.

Alone among the huge white dunes.

The Good, the Bad, and Kafka

THE DOORBELL RINGS. In a section of the city that has electricity. I'm in that part of town, in an apartment with a functioning doorbell. Alone. I open the door.

"Good day," he says.

He takes off his hat. His eyes are black like raven feathers. He's slight and frail. I've never seen him before.

"Good day," I reply.

"I hear you're looking for me," he utters slowly, laboriously.

I'm looking for him? The hat twitches in his long, gnarled fingers. I invite him inside. He's a proper gentleman; he wipes his shoes on the doormat, several times. He stands timidly in the hallway, not knowing which side to enter. I open the door to the dining room.

"Come in, come in."

He must be some foreigner, I think. In the distance a grenade explodes. His entire body shudders. Fear is written in his pupils.

"Where are we?"

"In Sarajevo."

"Sarajevo?"

"Grbavica. That's the name of this neighborhood."

"Ah."

A burst of gunfire. Bullets hurtle through the air like bloated birds.

"There's a war on," I say.

"Which?"

"Which what?"

"Which war?"

"Well ours, in Bosnia."

"Sarajevo, Bosnia, war . . ."

He coughs. Forcefully. Painfully. He's pale, exceedingly so. I bring him a glass of water from the kitchen. He thanks me.

"Pardon me, but why are you looking for me in this war?"

"You're Franz, is that right?"

He nods.

"And you?"

"I'm Lejla."

"Lejla from Grbavica."

"No, no, this is my grandparents' apartment. Grandma and I came back here so I could cross to the other side."

"Other side?"

"Other part of town. Where Nana and Papa live."

"Ah."

Tumult below the window. Sirens. The sound of boots pounding the asphalt.

"You mean, this isn't your house? Your house is on the other side?"

I lean against the table. I gesture for him to come closer.

I whisper, "This is my house too. But you see, around here the bad guys are in charge."

"Bad guys?"

"Shhhhh," I breathe, bringing my finger to my lips.

"And where is your grandmother?"

"At our downstairs neighbor's. They're baking bread."

I go to the kitchen and return with a bowl of kifle, our crescent rolls.

"Take one. They were made yesterday."

Franz thanks me and takes a kifla. He chews slowly. With difficulty. He coughs again. I take the bowl back from him.

"Why aren't you having any?" he asks.

"Nah, I'm on a diet."

He laughs. Crumbs fall from his mouth.

"How old are you?"

"Fourteen, in a few days."

"And you're on a diet?"

"On the other side everybody's thin. So I want to be thin. To fit in."

"Ah."

Now he leans against the table. I move closer to him.

"Who is over there? On the other side?"

"The good guys are there."

"So, here the bad guys, there the good guys, and it's war."

I nod my head.

"And you want to be there, with the good guys?"

"I want to be home. With Nana and Papa."

He's only eaten half the kifla. He takes a few sips of water. Looks around the dining room.

"How will you get there?"

"Via the Blue Route."

"What's that?"

"A bridge. That's where the border is, where you can cross."

"Then why don't you go?"

"First they'd have to let me."

"Who?"

"The bad guys."

"Ah."

We fall silent.

I'm hungry, so I take a kifla. I bite off a big piece, chew quickly, and say, "You know, there are good ones here too."

"And who are they?"

"They're the good bad ones. They'll help me leave on the Blue Route."

"Ah."

"Just yesterday a good bad guy came and brought me to an office where they have a ham radio. He left me alone to talk with my dad."

"Well he's good then."

"A good bad guy, I tell you."

I take another kifla. Franz says nothing.

"The thing is this," I whisper, "if I were to cross over to where the good ones are, someone from there would have to come over here."

"Who?"

"I don't know, I guess a bad good guy."

He eyes me. In his eyes glows a spark of warmth.

"Who are you?"

"Well, Lejla, I told you."

"Fine, but who are you? A good one, a bad one, a bad good one, a good bad one?"

"What do I know? Here I am with the bad guys, but I want to be with the good guys. It may be that I'm a good bad one, or a bad good one."

"Mmm. And why are you looking for me in this war?"

"Because I read your novel."

"I see."

He rises from his chair. Trembles on shaky legs. He heads for the balcony door. Grasps the doorknob.

"No!" I yell.

Franz starts. He freezes in place.

"Don't open the door. There are snipers."

"Who?"

"Snipers. Soldiers."

"Where from?"

"From the Executive Council."

"Where's that?"

"On the other side."

Franz parts the curtains and peeks out.

"You mean, good snipers?"

"Ah."

I take another kifla. Chew. Swallow.

"Who are they shooting at?"

"Whoever's there," I mumble with a full mouth.

The curtains fall back into place. Franz turns toward me. He sits at the table. Watches me. He nonchalantly hands me the bowl of kifle.

"So you were saying?"

"What was I saying?"

"What did you read?"

"*The Trial.*"

"At your age?"

"What am I supposed to do, I'm bored, I can't go out because of the snipers. And our neighbor Zora has a lot of books. Her apartment is unoccupied. Our neighbor Rada has a key. She told me I could take something to read."

"And you chose *The Trial*?"

"First I took *The Red and the Black*."

"How did you like it?"

"Not bad. Pleasant enough."

"Ah."

"It took a long time to read. Thick book. Then I took *The Trial*, because it was thinner."

"And?"

"And what?"

"How was it?"

"Awful!"

There's one kifla left. I push the bowl in front of Franz.

"You take it. I ate almost all of them."

"No, no, just eat."

We fall silent.

"Hence, you're looking for me so you can tell me my book is awful."

I laugh.

He smiles.

"And me? Am I also awful?"

I laugh even louder.

"No, seriously. What am I: bad, good, bad good, good bad?"

"You're crazy! How can you write such things? An innocent man suffering like that. For no reason. I mean, really. How did you come up with it?"

Franz puts on his hat. He checks his watch.

"It's late already."

He coughs.

"And I don't feel very well."

Outside, the blasts of several explosions in a row. Franz rises from the table. He gazes at me with his sad, deep eyes, the color of raven feathers.

Call Me Esteban

MY FIRST POSTWAR summer at the seaside. Me and my seven-year-old cousin Haris, who's never been to the coast before. It's a school trip to Mali Drvenik. The rest of the first-graders are accompanied by their mothers, but Haris has brought me. Fuck it, there was no other option. His mother, Melida, works at the supermarket, with no days off, no weekends. We all live on her paycheck and Papa's pension. We'll pay for the trip in installments. It's important for Haris to go with his friends and their teacher.

I'm in my first year of college. Philosophy, literature. Here I'm staying in a big room that smells like lavender. I've packed more books than underwear. Everything I read accumulates in my brain like a rain cloud poised to pour down and then evaporate in the heat of the day.

At the beach, the mothers hang out in a pack. They drink coffee, eat ice cream, shout at their children. They talk and talk. When they notice me with a book in my hand they smile blandly, wistfully. I don't understand their smiles. I smile shyly back at them, then bury my gaze in the pages. I contemplate one particular mother who lost her son.

It was in the film *All About My Mother*. The mother, Manuela, had her Esteban, who was killed by a car on his birthday. Esteban had wanted to write a novel about his mother, but Almodóvar made a film about the mother mourning her son. I saw the film at the Meeting Point Cinema. That evening I went home right after. I walked through the old part of town, toward my motherless house. The figure of Esteban vibrated before my eyes. I saw him there, drenched in his jeans and windbreaker, clutching his soggy notebook. The street I was trudging up was called Širokac, and it was incredibly steep. At the top I paused to catch my breath, and turned to face the valley. The city below was sinking into darkness, and it occurred to me: What if my mother were still alive today, and it had been me who'd died that faraway night seventeen years before?

The sun is sizzling on the beach. The mothers sit fanning themselves under a clutch of pine trees. Sweat drips down their necks, their thighs glistening, their voices hushed. The children run wild on the hot pebbles. They pelt each other, chase each other; their teacher yells at them. Every now and then some kid wades into the shallow water without permission, soaking his arms and legs, then turning toward the shore and sticking out his tongue at the others. The teacher races to him; the mothers shout.

Dreams crystallize into salt on skin. I read Márquez. Short stories. One of them is called "The Handsomest Drowned Man in the World." My forehead wrinkles when I realize he too is named Esteban. The sun surrenders the protective zone of the umbrella. The beach mat drinks the sweat from my skin. I take a pen from my backpack and circle every mention of his name: Esteban, Esteban, Esteban . . . The blue ink dries instantly, isolating the seven-letter word like police tape at a crime scene.

Gabo's Esteban is dressed in algae and shells, enveloped in the scent of the sea. Who knows how long the water carried him. His corpse washed up at the coastal village that would become his hallowed grave. I touch my palm to my neck. It's blazing. Painful. I should cover up. Without thinking, I stare directly into the sun. Fiery and white, the type that shines only in the south, it upends my perspective. It flips just like Almodóvar's camera immediately after we hear the dull thud of the young man's body against the windshield of the luxury sedan. Manuela's running, the rhythm of her heels hitting the pavement, pulsates through my thoughts.

When the moment of blindness passes, I behold my dead body on the surface of the sea. Gentle waves drag it along, like a refined horse trying to tow a hearse at a trot. Once I'm delivered to the shallows, the children notice me. They abandon their fighting and teasing. The pebbles slip from their hands. They come running. They gape at me, grab my nose, yank my hair, stick their small fingers in my ears. They tear at my algae, pour sand in my open mouth, pound my chest. Playful, euphoric, they attract their mothers' attention. When the women detect the dead toy amidst their children's little bodies, they take off running breathlessly. Every last one of them sprints to us, shredding their bare feet on the beach's sharp stones. Their long, gauzy dresses are buoyed by the water, floating around their hips like multicolored seaweed. The mothers rip the leeches from my hands, remove the tangled strands of hair from my face. With flustered voices they order their children: "Hurry, get her!"

She wears a white dress that makes her hair and brows seem even blacker. Everyone falls silent at the sound of her footsteps. The children and their mothers move back. Lightly but decisively she approaches my body. Her creased face leans over mine. The sun is radiating. She takes my head and cradles it in her hands, like an egg in a nest. She is my mother. On the cusp of old age. She lowers her lips to my eyes, then licks a salty droplet from my lashes. "This is Esteban!" she says. The rest of the women exchange surprised looks. "Esteban, and no one else!" she cries. Upon hearing this, the other women gather around me again. They begin to wail in unison. They rake their faces, pull their hair, rend their dresses. "It's Esteban!" declares my mother once more, kissing my blue cheeks. All the other women stand, nodding. Like a flock of nervous birds, they surround my mother. I feel the tears in her warm, wet kisses. The rest join her in hugging me, kissing every part of my body. Time drifts along; the sun slides toward the horizon.

And that's that. An impeccable death, perfectly suited to me.

Had I Met You

AT DUSK, I walk through the park behind the high school, Druga Gimnazija. I take a seat on a bench and breathe in the scent of freshly cut grass. The large park in the center of the city is rather empty. My ideal spot for killing an evening. Cars glide along Koševo and Alipašina Streets. I grab a bottle of water from my backpack. Ice cold, from the refrigerator in the newsstand at the beginning of Aleksina Street. I bought it and a pack of Yorks. I tear off the plastic sheath and pull out a cigarette while my other hand fumbles for the lighter in my jeans.

"Can you spare one?"

I raise my head. Her voice is softer than mine. Her hair, shorter than mine. Our smiles are alike. I nod and hold out the pack. She takes a cigarette, looking at me. I raise the lighter to her face. From the gas springs the little flame. Animated. She quickly inhales, once, twice, then thanks me. I move down the bench a little. She sits close to me, winks at me, and taps me on the shoulder. As if we just saw each other yesterday. A lingering trace of summer. We smoke in silence.

"Your school?"

She's wearing a waist-length suede jacket, Levis, and dirty canvas sneakers with white rubber cap toes.

"Yes. That there," I say, pointing, "is the faculty room. Next to it is the chemistry lab, at least it was when I went there. Below it is the history classroom, above it, geography."

The smoke wafts between our bodies; the cigarette embers pulsate like the tiny hearts of two different worlds. Is this how I imagined her?

"So, what's up?" she says, tapping my shoulder again, smiling.

I shrug. "Nothing, the usual."

Her hands are different from mine. She follows my eyes. Gently takes my fingers in her hand.

"You have his hands."

"It seems like I have his everything."

A Mercedes blocks the street. Everyone honks, seething on the asphalt. We stand to get a better look.

"Look at the traffic on Kralja Tomislava Street."

"Koševo."

"Huh?"

"It's called Koševo now."

She looks over at the other side.

"Đure Đakovića Street?"

"Alipašina."

"And this park?"

"Park Svjetlosti."

We sit back down. Fall silent.

"Anyway," she says, "how is he?"

"I don't know, better than he used to be, I guess."

She has a pretty smile.

"Do you see each other? Talk?"

"Sometimes."

She smokes and gazes ahead.

"He goes up to visit you," I say.

"Does he?"

"Usually he calls me when he gets back. Last time he told me a vase had broken at the bottom, next to the bench. The one that Grandma and Grandpa had plugged with chewing gum so the water wouldn't leak. He plants flowers now."

"Menso? No way!"

"The man threw himself into horticulture. It calms him down."

She smiles. I take a sip of water. I offer her some, but she doesn't want it.

"He remarried, did you know?"

A woman on a balcony across the street from the park hangs up her laundry. White T-shirts, sheets, and pillowcases flap in the breeze, like flags.

"Does it bother you?" she asks.

I shake my head.

"You?"

She shakes her head too. Smiles.

"I have a brother and a sister."

"You're kidding! What are they like?"

"Little . . . blond . . . funny . . . I don't know."

We smoke. The sun sets somewhere in the distance.

"Do you ever go up?" She gestures in the direction of Bare.

"I haven't in a while, but Papa is always insisting."

"Nedžad, he's still alive?"

"Uh-huh, he's the last of the four of them. He nags me non-stop: 'You should go, she gave birth to you.'"

"You live at his place?"

"Yes. Me, him, Aunt Melida."

"My little Melić? How is she?"

"Okay. She's grown up. Has a son. He's almost eight. He's blond too. We're a family now. Papa, Melida, her Haris, and me."

I sense a warmth in her eyes.

"And Papa nonstop: 'Why don't you go up there? Take your girlfriend along. It's quite a promenade in the evenings.' Can you believe what he comes up with—that I should take girlfriends for walks in the cemetery! He says: 'What's the problem, there are lovely paths there, and flowers too. It smells wonderful. And boy is it peaceful.'"

We laugh to the point of tears. The noise disturbs the sparrows; every last one of them flees the bushes near our bench. I follow their short flight.

"Oh, Nećko, Nećko." She shakes her head. "Anyway, what about you?"

"What do you mean?"

"Well, those girlfriends, and such."

The earth could swallow me up. I know, it's completely normal for a mother to ask, but I just can't spill my guts.

"What girlfriends?"

She grins at me, just like my grandmother used to.

"Really, there's nothing to tell. I'm studying for some exams, stuff like that."

The sky darkens, and cars continue to pass.

"There's something I've never told anyone."

"What?" she asks.

"It's silly."

"Come on, tell me."

"Shortly after you died Menso bought a burial plot next to yours. For himself. He built a headstone too."

"You don't say?"

"But then life happened."

"It's not so easy to die either," she says knowingly.

"He's got a new wife, so logically he won't be buried there. And we have a problem."

"Huh?"

"Papa came back from the cemetery once in a pensive mood. I asked him what was wrong, and he said, about Menso's plot: 'They made it, and we're still paying for it. But who'll be buried in an atheist grave now?'"

I burst out laughing again.

"How come?" she asks, confused.

"Well, you know: Kralja Tomislava—Koševo; Đure Đakovića—Alipašina; Hasana Brkića—Patriotske lige. There was a war. A total shitstorm."

It's still not entirely clear to her, but she keeps listening.

"So I see that Nedžad has worked out something he's reluctant to say: 'What would you think . . . if we gave it to Rada?'"

"Who?"

"Rada's our neighbor. Nećko figured she's a Serb, so it's all the same to her. This way it won't go to waste."

"What happened?"

"Nothing. I told him not to say a word. But he persists: 'What's the matter. It would be so nice for her there. I'd give it to her for free. Do you know how much it costs to be buried these days?'"

"Then what will you do with it?"

"No idea. We'll find someone eventually."

From laughter flows silence, and from silence, emptiness. The lights glow throughout the park. We stare at each other. Her eyes are black, clear like the arriving night.

"It's late," she says, rising.

I reach for another cigarette, search for my lighter.

"Don't smoke so much, it's not good for you," she says, touching the tip of her forefinger to my nose and winking.

We look at each other.

"I need to get going."

"Okay."

I stand to see her off. The darkness has brought a stronger wind. She buttons my jacket. Lifts my collar. Tidies me up.

"And you?" she asks.

"What about me?"

"What will you do now?"

I shrug. We stand there a long time. One facing the other.

"Maybe one day I'll write a story about your death."

An Appeal to Elizabeth

DEAR ELIZABETH,

I'm writing to you because I don't know what else to do. You once wrote: "The art of losing isn't hard to master." Here in the psychiatric hospital I've lost all sense of time. I only know there's so much of it that I have no idea whether tomorrow will even come. I'm writing (please excuse me if I'm bothering you) because I've decided to lose everything. I would like to keep only my mind. But given how things are going, I may not be able to keep that either.

I didn't want to lose people, or things, or my sense of time. It just happened. I lost my mother, but I didn't know it for a long time. When they finally told me, I think I was about five years old. They believed that it was the right time. I was completely fine with it. Then the country I lived in lost its peace. Which caused my family to lose its peace too. When it finally returned, it was too late for my grandparents. They died. With them my mother died a second death. But again, I was okay with it. I hadn't known her, and they'd been old. The houses we lived in died with them too. And that too was okay. Fuck the houses. But when the houses died, the times we lived in died as well. Having lost those times, I was ultimately hospitalized.

The doctors didn't believe me when I told them I was okay with everything that had happened. "That's not right, that's not normal," they said. Since it was no longer clear to me what was normal and what wasn't (I was a little out of it from the medication), I once blurted out, "If Elizabeth could lose her mother, and later Lota, and whatnot, and she was fine, then I'm fine too." They sent me for tests. They measured various components of my blood, they analyzed my thyroid function, they read my brainwaves. They eventually concluded that my body wasn't the problem.

My illness was diagnosed to be the consequence of losing my mother, my closest relatives, the houses (two), and my sense of time. My mind had bizarrely signaled to me that this was okay. The treatment consists of 10 mg Zyprexa every evening, 20 mg Seroxat every morning, and 5mg Apaurin three times a day. At these dosages the state of my mind is the same, except that the world passes by much more slowly. I'm always in a kind of limbo between wakefulness and sleep. Often I recite "One Art" to myself. Since I've lost all sense of time, I don't know how long it takes me to get from one line to the next.

Mostly I lie in bed. I stare at the ceiling, surrounded by silence and the sense that all the cities of the world have floated away from me. In the sessions with my doctor I talk about you, your poems. The meds make my speech slow; the doctor typically smokes four or five cigarettes while I'm in her office. Yesterday I told her about Lota, that she'd been in a psych ward, and later killed herself. The doctor asked then whether I wanted to kill myself. I told her I've lost all sense of what death is.

At every session we talk about death. The doctor asks me if I go to the cemetery. I tell her I haven't been there in years, that

LEJLA KALAMUJIĆ

it doesn't interest me. We don't agree on much, but especially not on the matter of the cemetery. She thinks that once I'm in a stable condition, I should go there. With flowers and tears. She says that my nightmares, the ones that predict a terrible flood swallowing up the cities, the cemeteries, and the bones of the dead, will stop then. She says that this flood, all murky and horrifyingly brown, actually represents my tears that—once I'm stable—need to flow into the soil of the graves. I listen to her, neither awake nor asleep. Sometimes she gets carried away and says I should think less about their bones feeding the soil and more about their souls in the sky. I haven't told her, but I can tell you, Elizabeth, that I've reflected on this and I've reached the conclusion that our souls are too heavy for the sky. The clouds would surely give way under the weight of their swollen feet.

Dear Elizabeth, it's dark now. I don't know whether night is falling or the poplar trees are blocking the sun. I only know that I've lost my sense of time and that my eyelids are swollen from the meds. I also know that you died a year before I was born. It was autumn. You're buried in Boston, Massachusetts. I've lost you too. In the end (if this is the end), my dear Eli, I need you to tell me just one thing: Have I mastered the art of losing?
    Sincerely,
    Lejla

The Sound, the Fury, and Her

I CAN'T SLEEP. If I roll over, I'll wake her. She's a light sleeper. Always has been. My restlessness woke her the first night. When I opened my eyes in the morning, she was sitting on the bed and watching me. "You slept terribly," she said, "gnashing your teeth, clenching your fists, muttering to yourself." As quietly as I can, I slide out from under the blanket. Kiki is curled up napping by her feet. At my movement she pricks up her ears, opens her eyes, and stretches out a paw. Yawns. I bring my finger to my lips. "Sleep, Kiki." I search for my slippers under the bed. Peek through the curtain. Outside, sound and fury. Jugovina, the warm wind that comes from the southeast, has arrived in Sarajevo. It whips through the treetops, whirls trash around the empty streets. A poor dog trembles next to a newsstand. Earlier I read about the severe weather in Croatia. It's scattered people, carried off roofs; sea swells are pounding the Dalmatian coast. I turn toward her. She's fine, sleeping. In the kitchen I hastily make coffee and light a cigarette. The ticking clock announces 2:30. Daybreak is far off. I pace the kitchen. My heart constricts with anxiety. I notice the glow of an unread message on my phone. Right now the lighthouses on the Adriatic must be speaking to one another this way, in the Bura. I read Nermina's words: "Wanna get coffee with me and Hana on Wednesday?"

* * *

The first morning, making the excuse that I had all sorts of things to do, I quickly left her apartment. The texts from Hana and Nermina came at me nonstop: questions, curiosity, teasing. Finally, we agreed to hang out at Nermina's that night. I was the last to arrive, and they'd prepared everything: coffee, cards, music. My only job was to talk. To spill my guts, down to the tiniest detail. But this time my typically pensive expression bothered them.

"Where is your smile? Why do you look like a soggy mushroom?"

What was I supposed to say—I recognized that it hadn't gone so well.

"C'mon, Lejla, it was the first time," Hana declared. "What did you expect?"

"No, not that part," I said, "but afterward."

I told them how my nightmares had woken her up, that it wasn't a good sign. Because this past of mine . . .

Nermina stopped listening to deal the cards, then launched into her usual, "Leli, you'd be better off forgetting all that!" We laughed. Hana wiped the floor with us at cards and kept pouring water into her coffee to dilute it. After a couple hours, she gazed into her cup and said, "I've been drinking this coffee the whole time, and the cup is still full!" We laughed some more. They looked at me, puzzled, their impatience growing. Especially Hana's. "Anyway, it's time to tell us everything. What happened? How was it?" Feeling more cheerful, more light-hearted, I started babbling. We talked late into the night over many hands of cards.

The storm is amplifying my inner cacophony. I peep out again: the whirlwind scares me. I look at the clock and continue pacing about. Kiki enters, blinking. I pour cat food into her dish. The kibble crunches between her sharp teeth. She licks her chops. I light another cigarette. She jumps into my lap and I cuddle her while she purrs. I write to Nermina: "Okay." I know she's sleeping, the sound and fury aren't crashing against the shore of her sleep, but I add: "It's a fucking mess outside."

* * *

I walked toward the meeting place. We'd agreed on seven. I didn't hurry, I had time. I considered: maybe Nermina was right. Maybe it was time to fucking get over myself and forget. After all, I'd survived the psych ward. I was here, on the street, on the outside. I was walking. Not thinking I'd collapse at the next step. Sky above me, earth below. They'd encouraged me last night. And my doctor had this morning.

I'd burst into her office without an appointment. Desk, white coat, typewriter. A bag of pumpkin seeds in her hand. I apologized for showing up outside our regular schedule and said I could wait out front if I was interrupting something. She smiled and said don't be silly, come on in. Then in a worried voice she asked if something had happened, had I run out of medicine? "No, no," I said. She offered me the pumpkin seeds, said she'd quit smoking and needed something to chew on. "No thank you," I said, waving them aside. I felt embarrassed, but the situation had compelled me to seek an expert opinion. So I told the doctor about her, our emails, our dates, and I recounted our first night together, while glancing up at the ceiling—I mean,

I didn't want to go on endlessly, but hey, she needed to know what had happened. I looked at her. She was chewing on the seeds, smiling. Now I felt even more embarrassed, so I stared out the window and prayed to heaven and earth that I wasn't blushing. I felt like smoking, but how could I, the woman had just quit. We sat in silence. I didn't know what to do, so I apologized again for popping in unannounced.

"What's the problem?" she asked.

"Look," I said, "the thing is . . . I'm not sure this is fair . . . I mean . . . you know how I was . . . I fell apart right before your eyes . . . and now . . ."

She interrupted me. "And now we're stable, in remission, aren't we?"

"Yes, we are. A year already."

"What does the girl say?"

I couldn't help but smile. "She . . . just looks at me with her blue eyes, like none of it matters. She says it doesn't bother her, that we can handle this."

"Then what's the problem?"

"You see . . . I mean . . . is it fair to drag her into all this? I mean . . . into what's left of me . . . What if I have another breakdown? What if the sound and fury come back?"

The doctor took me by the arm: this was her way of averting an attack of my doubts and fears. She fixed her gaze on me, then mechanically offered me the bag of pumpkin seeds. Jeez woman, I wanted to scream, I don't want your damn seeds! But I only smiled weakly.

"You too have the right to be loved," she said.

Eh, fuck it. I was as red as a fresh wound. I saw that she thought my embarrassment was endearing, but I pretended not to understand. Suddenly I stood up, thanked her, and apologized again for coming by with no notice. The doctor swiveled

LEJLA KALAMUJIĆ

her chair toward the window, pushing a seed between her teeth, and, more to herself than me, muttered, "Such is life."

I spotted her in the distance. Hat, vest, umbrella in her hand. I paused. Passersby wondered at my smiling. I wished I could just stand there gazing at her. She glanced at her watch, a little nervous. I approached her. Some powerful force pulled me toward her. The happiness in her eyes when she would see me. She asked where I wanted to go. Somewhere without a lot of people. "You know," I said carefully, "crowds still don't agree with me." That was fine with her.

We sat in a café. There were only the two of us, and the waitress sitting at the bar. We chatted quietly, drawing closer together. She timidly asked if everything was okay, since I'd left so quickly the day before. I knew the time had come. I stood up, put on my jacket, and said, "I need to show you something."

The wind blew tiny raindrops at our faces. We walked down Zagrebačka Street in silence. Arriving at the building, we climbed up one flight. I unlocked the door. I turned on the light in the empty, abandoned apartment.

"Where are we?" she asked.

"In my past."

She pivoted, regarding the damp, stained walls with confusion.

"This is my grandma and grandpa's apartment."

She asked me where they were now.

"Dead," I said. I grabbed a box from the corner of the room and placed it in the middle, inviting her to sit. "You see, I betrayed them. They died in another city. Alone."

She didn't ask anything more. I reached for another box and sat on it beside her. We were silent. She took my hand and placed it in her palm. The polish on my fingernails was cracked. I tried to withdraw my hand, but she wouldn't let me. I explained: "Nermina and Hana did my nails the other night. I couldn't stop them. They went to half the cosmetics stores in the city to find decent clear polish. I kindly told them not to bother. Not for me. Everything breaks on me."

She placed my hand on her cheek. Kissed it. "How did the apartment look before?" she asked with genuine curiosity.

No one's eyes had ever penetrated me like hers. And I'd been gazed upon by the lost, the screwed, the angry, the happy, the weepy, the psychotic. Her gaze went all the way to my bones, entered my most remote places.

"Here was the sofa, canvas, in three colors," I gestured toward the wall. Her smile encouraged me to continue. "The dining table was here, and three chairs, for the three of us."

I led her across the hallway into another room, then into the kitchen. My words sketched a lost world. She listened. How well she knew how to listen.

* * *

For ten years we've been coming here. We enter the hollow insides of my childhood. She helps me clean the floors. She runs over here with me when they call me about the flooding, when black water leaks down the neighbor's walls. She stands beside me while I apologize. She stands beside me when my old neighbors stall me and ask, "Lejla, honey, why don't you move in?" And I reply, for who knows how many years now, "I can't. I don't have the papers. I'm not allowed." I just have a key and a pile of memories I don't know where to put. She nods when they curse these times and this government: "Because, darling, you were all they had." And she removed the splinter that drove itself into my finger once when I tried to fix the holes in the rotted window frames.

I return to the bedroom as quietly as I can. I stand at the window. Down in front of the building, the moon's reflection creases in a puddle. She jerks awake and sits up in bed, calling for me.

"I'm right here. Sleep," I say.

She can't, she's awake, a little frightened.

"Should I leave?" I ask.

"What's up with you again?" she asks.

"I was scared, look at the storm. What if the windows don't hold. The glass could break. Should I put tape around the edges? Who knows what kind of damage the wind could do."

She calls me by name. I sit at the edge of the bed. She hugs me from behind. "Everything's all right," she whispers. She says that in the morning we'll go outside together, check everything, fix whatever needs fixing. And now I should lie down, I can't stay up all night. Here's Kiki, curling back up in her place. I crawl under the blanket. I kiss her. She hugs me in return, and I nestle more tightly against her body, against her image of the world. I inhale her scent and realize that life doesn't always give you what you deserve. Because I did nothing to deserve her. Outside the lightning flashes and the thunder peals, but I sink into sleep, a little more convinced that I did, in fact, survive.

On the Art of Breathing

"YOU ASLEEP?"

"How can I sleep when you turn like a propeller."

"Sorry, I'll stop."

"What is it now?"

"I was making sure you were breathing."

"Oh no, not again!"

"What?"

"I'm breathing normally, what's wrong with you? I need to sleep. You know I have work in the morning!"

"Oh, really? I had no idea."

I fall silent.

"Now you're the one who's angry."

"No, I'm not."

"Come on, tell me."

"Tell you what?"

"How would you like me to breathe?"

"Normally."

"Normally how?"

"Just normally, with your chest visibly rising, so I don't have to stare at your head waiting to see a hair move. I'll fucking go blind."

"I'll go crazy. I can't control my breathing!"

"And I can control my fears?"

"It's a problem when I breathe slowly, and it's a problem when I breathe fast."

"Don't mock me."

"While I was on the step machine, you came into the room ten times!"

"You were panting, it sounded like you might croak."

"I was exercising, hello!"

"You have no limits. You were straining so much I could hear you gasping all the way from the kitchen."

"It's cardio! That's what's supposed to happen!"

"So you're a workout expert now. You can't even kick a ball. Haven't you ever heard of people overdoing it, even elite athletes? Do you want to die of a heart attack?"

"I'm not going to die of a heart attack, understand?"

"No of course, I understand everything."

"Did you see your psychiatrist this morning?"

"What does that have to do with anything?"

"Did you?"

"Yes."

"And?"

"And what?"

"What did she say about your crazy fears?"

"That I should learn to live with them."

"There, you see, the woman knows what she's talking about. Now go to sleep, I have a meeting in the morning."

"You sleep. I'm going to stay up a little longer."

"What is it now?"

"Just so you know, you're being unfair."

"How am I being unfair?"

"Look. You didn't even touch it."

"You know I don't like honey."

"I went all over the fucking city to find the kind made from pine needles."

"I hate honey!"

"And I hate your bronchial flare-ups, when your lungs shriek and wheeze as if you've swallowed a sick canary!"

"So you want me to take it?"

"I do!"

"You seriously do?"

"Yes."

"Fine."

"What is it now?"

"I'll throw up."

"You do this to me on purpose!"

"I really am sick."

"I'm sick of your wheezing."

"Okay, I swallowed some honey. Are you happy now?"

"Yes."

We fall silent.

"You sleeping?"

"I'm not sleeping."

"Come here."

"Go to sleep. You need to be up early."

"You're still upset."

"No I'm not."

"Yes you are, you are."

"Stop, I'm not in the mood."

"What is it now?"

"I can't. I'm tired. So tired. I know my behavior's absurd. But I can't control it. These fears."

"Shhh."

"What if I lost you too?"

"Hey, everything's okay. We're okay. Kiki's here. Relax."
"Goodnight."
"Nighty-night."
"Sweetie, where's Kiki?"
"Under my legs."
"What's she doing?"
"Sleeping, what else?"
"Okay."
 She falls silent.
"Sweetie."
"What now?"
"I can't hear her breathing."

Bella Ciao

FORGIVE ME. I know it took me too long. I'm sorry it's too late. I went up there. I was at your place. But I want to tell you more than that. I need to tell you everything.

I was ten years old. A sultry afternoon. Nana was teary, Papa seething, because who knows how many times they'd nagged Dad to stop going to the bar. They'd been begging him to remarry. They wouldn't live forever, after all. What would become of them? Of me? But they were whistling in the wind. You know my dad, he didn't listen to anyone. To me it was all the same. My toys, my bike, the neighborhood awaited me. Papa gave me some money for the store in Mejdan, I bought chocolate and chips, and—I almost ran right into you. You were holding a shopping bag, chatting with an old man I'd seen around. I watched you out of the corner of my eye, so you wouldn't notice. I thought: it would be super if Dad married you! Never before and never since have I thought this about anyone. But it felt so normal to want to be near you.

I couldn't shake the memory of you: the next day, the day after that, the days that followed. I found out your name. The grownups mentioned you sometimes, but I didn't understand what they were talking about. The atmosphere at home was enlivened by my aunt's upcoming marriage. Everyone was bustling about, making plans. One morning, two days before the wedding, Nana was breathlessly unloading her bags, pulling out cheese and sour cream for uštipci, those yummy little balls of fried dough. She remarked to Auntie that she'd seen you. I didn't move: I stuffed a big piece of uštipak in my mouth and listened. She said you'd promised to come to the wedding and bring musicians along.

On the big day, my stomach hurt. I felt ill, and no one knew it was from excitement at the prospect of seeing you. They thought it was because Auntie was leaving me, because she was like a big sister to me. I put on my new pants and a red shirt with a white lace collar. I even let Nana put a barrette in my hair. Just one, just this once, for you. Dancing, singing, drinking. It didn't even bother anyone that Dad was hitting the bottle—it was a celebration. The hours passed, with no sight of you. Maybe you'd gotten lost? You couldn't find the building? Every now and then I snuck outside. I sauntered along, peering into the alleyways, and climbed to the top of Logavina Street. I stood there, looking for you. I went to sleep just before dawn, on the sofa in the guest room. The next day, it occured to me: you must've forgotten. It wasn't important. The wedding wasn't all that great, and the marriage didn't last long. And today I still firmly believe that if you'd been there, the party would've been a hundred times better.

I begged Dad to bring me along to one of the taverns where I thought I might see you. Papa approved it, thinking we were going for ćevapi at Željo's and cake at Egipat. I promised I wouldn't say a word about visiting bars like Kod Piketa, or sometimes Čarli, where they had framed posters of Chaplin on the walls. We would sit, Dad's pals would come and go, and whenever he'd say it was time to get going, I'd order one more juice. Who knows, I thought, you might show up unexpectedly.

Then the war came and I believed our paths would never cross again. I heard you were in Slovenia, that you were performing up there, that you were doing well.

We ran into one another in '97 or '98, again in Mejdan. You'd come back! Dad had remarried in the meantime, but I no longer cared about that. I'd come to understand you. To understand myself. I peeked at you building your new house. Brick by brick, alone, with your own hands. I was happy. With every new layer of brick the pain I'd felt when someone had snickered at you receded. Bella, no matter how long you kept quiet, they knew. But you know what, fuck them! They pointlessly faked their building permits, locked their gates to hide the two-story houses sprouting in their gardens; in vain they erected new fences and sturdier roofs. They couldn't protect themselves from the sun or the clouds. They couldn't do anything. You built the most beautiful house, with the loveliest view of the city.

Sometimes I'd walk down your street, as if unwittingly. Acting like I was in a hurry, I would constantly check my watch. It's funny to me now, because I know you knew perfectly well that I didn't hurry anywhere, that I had nowhere to be. So many times I wanted to ask: What was it like for you? Where did you hang out? Where did you go? One time, I gathered up some courage and lingered a bit near your house. I lit a cigarette and gazed out at the city. Suddenly, something creaked. Your front door opened, and I caught sight of you taking out the trash. I chuckled from panic and stared at Vijećnica like I'd never seen it before. In an instant you looked at me, and I looked back as if by accident. You nodded in a sign of greeting, turned, and went back inside. The door closed.

That night, as usual, I played cards with Nermina and Hana. Something had thawed in me. I emphatically proclaimed the sunset beyond compare. The hours passed, and I blabbered on and on.

Them: "Deal the cards."

Me: "Just look at the sky's purple undertones."

Them: "Come on, deal."

Me: "And the bridges over the Miljacka, what a sheen they acquire at twilight."

When I said, "The tram glided past Vijećnica with unprecedented ease. What masterful steering!" Nermina threw down her cards.

"For God's sake, what the fuck is up with you tonight?"

I didn't know. They told me seven days later. You'd died, and I hadn't been there. They told me it was cancer, and the diagnosis came too late. They said, "Just two months," and I had to take their word that you didn't suffer too much, and that you went in your sleep.

What can I tell you now? About life? About the city? They say the time to fight will come. I know it will. But every once in a while, I encounter someone older, someone in whom I see you. At first, they look at me gloomily and warily. I long to ask them: Where did your love blossom? Which hidden passageways were yours, which buildings, which curtains gave you cover? I understand the fear in their eyes. And that they're pretending not to see me, not to hear me. That they take care not to let our bodies touch inadvertently in passing. I understand. I learned the language of silence. They too are alone, you know, and I have no one to ask whether ultimately that's how it is? Bella, I'm scared of solitude.

I hadn't been up there in a while. I thought I never would again. When some poets from Sweden came to Sarajevo this summer and it was my job to take them around, I couldn't help but show them the most beautiful view of the city. We stood a little uphill from your house, under an old walnut tree. They took pictures, delighting in the panorama. I moved closer and leaned against the wall you'd built with your own hands. I wanted the asphalt to crack, I wanted a wild rosebush to spring up and bind my feet, the walnut tree to lower its branches and embrace me. I wanted to stay there as long as possible.

"Who lives here?" asked one of the poets.

"No one," I said.

She looked at me, expecting me to continue, but I didn't want to go into it, not even with a Swede. Night was falling. I reminded them that we should get going, it wouldn't be good to arrive late to our event.

Ciao, my Bella! The years pass. Bella, ciao! I don't know whether other worlds exist. I have no answers. But I swear to you I'll remember you madly. However long I can, whenever I can. Because you must know: you being there made it easier for me. Know this, too: people will pass by. They'll come better and braver than I. They'll snap photos, they'll admire it. With your eyes they'll see the city. "What a lovely house," they'll say. They will, Bella, they will.

The Milky Way

I HAD AN OWL. I named her Sky. She was a gift from Uncle Ranko, Grandpa's bald older friend from work, an excellent hunter.
Sky lived above the door in the hallway. She perched on a piece of
beautifully carved and lacquered beechwood. Her talons, thick
and sharp, were firmly attached to the wood. Her eyes were dark
and dense. Large beak, with two holes in it. Stiff feathers, brown-
ish, spiked with yellow. She watched me day and night. So in-
tensely that sometimes I'd imagine that everyone I knew was
observing me through her dead eyes. And I watched her, often.
I'd lie on the hallway rug, prop my head in my hands, and wonder
about her life. Uncle Ranko told me, "I killed her with the first
shot." In the woods near Sarajevo. He bound her legs with rope,
turned her upside down, and tied her to his belt. He carried her
back to the city that way, shedding droplets of blood.

Ranko had another hobby. He loved taxidermy. Grandpa took
me to his workshop. I watched how he plucked the feathers from
a duck, peeled off its skin, scraped its meat from the bones, threw
the fat in the trash. The next time I visited, the dead duck's eyes
glittered. I declared that I wanted a hobby like Ranko's when I
grew up. Ranko often came over to our apartment in Grbavica.

Sometimes for lunch, other times for coffee and rakija. He would regale me with tales of his adventures.

I think it was autumn. I know it was pouring rain and I couldn't play ball. I lay beneath Sky with my arms crossed. Grandma was making apple cake, and Grandpa was listening to the game at Koševo on his transistor radio. I opened the door and loudly inquired: "Why didn't you stuff Mama when she died? We could've found a nice spot for her here, or in the bedroom. Ranko could've strung the wires through her bones, filled her with grass and straw, and sewn her up. Put soil in her eye sockets." I pulled two marbles from my pocket. "Or painted these black and put them in," I said, holding the marbles over my closed eyelids.

Maybe Mama really could've been like Sky, I kept thinking. For a couple weeks, Grandma and Grandpa watched me questioningly. They seemed relieved only when I burst into tears listening to "The Little Match Girl."

Ranko didn't come by anymore. Grandpa went over to his place instead, but would never take me along. I don't know what happened to him during the war, whether he survived. Sky disappeared, along with all the other things from our apartment.

I never would've thought of this again had I not stumbled on a group of children in a dead-end street on Vratnik this fall. They'd formed a circle, muttering to each other. I recognized one of them, and asked him with a smile what they were hiding. Like a bird opening its wings, the children separated. A blond, freckled kid in the middle held something in his palm. I drew closer. In the nest of the boy's hand sat a tiny owl. A third of the size of my Sky. It looked at me just like Sky had all those years. "She's blind," they whispered.

I drew closer to her dense, black eyes where, instead of pupils, there floated yellowish dots, like stars cast out of a constellation. I touched her beak with my nose. In those orbs roared the entire galaxy.

LEJLA KALAMUJIĆ

From Locomotive to Locomotive

Locomotive 1

ON DECEMBER 13, 2009, all the media outlets in the former Yugoslavia announced the revival of the train from Sarajevo to Belgrade. The line had been out of operation for eighteen years, and interest in the story led journalists in the ensuing days to write about passengers and their stories. The articles overflowed the borders of the former constituent republics, spreading to all corners of the earth. About ten travelers set out from Sarajevo on December 22, and I was among them. I headed to Šid, the Vojvodina border town where my grandmother had grown up. Her sister still lived in the area with her family. We hadn't seen each other since '94, when, after a ceasefire in Sarajevo, I'd decided to end my exile and return to the city.

I'm alone in the compartment. The train slowly pulls out of the Sarajevo station, the locomotive accelerating. Through the smudged window appear tall buildings. Like planted spears they rip through the swelling clouds. Grayness chews the first winter snow and spits it onto the muddy streets. I'm nervous: fifteen years is a long time. So is the eight hours of rattling along the ancient tracks. I take off my shoes and lie down. I make a pillow of my thick down jacket. I look around the compartment:

everything's the same, just eighteen years older. In its former days the train was called The Olympic Express.

How it was back then! Fast, and so long it stretched far beyond my child's view. It carried hundreds of passengers. In the former country they'd called it "the train of the future." Grandma, Grandpa, and I would take it to Šid every August. I still remember the blue lunch packs: sandwich, juice box, a yellow plastic knife wrapped in a soft paper napkin. I kept the bags in my room like other kids collected pebbles and shells on the beach.

Just before Zenica, the door opens. The conductor enters the compartment. White shirt, navy pants, cap on his head, black bag hanging from his shoulder. I hand him my ticket, he thanks me, inspects it carefully, runs a finger over it.

"To Šid?" he asks.

"To Šid," I reply.

He returns the ticket, wishes me a good trip, and leaves. I open the window; it gets stuck halfway. I smoke and gaze out at the surrounding houses. The wind pierces my eyes and nostrils. The old train and rusty suburbs cling to one another. The first traces of fog thicken the air. I close the window and lie back down.

Locomotive 2

A dull thud awakens me. The train car shakes. Drowsy, I peek into the hallway. Not a soul. The train has stopped. I go to the window, trying to see through the fog. I recognize Doboj. The rail workers unhook the locomotive of the Federation of Bosnia and Herzegovina and pull it onto another track. Then they haul over the locomotive of Republika Srpska. Connecting it

LEJLA KALAMUJIĆ

to the first car takes about twenty minutes. The train's wheels screech in the darkness. We set off. I get a text message from my great aunt asking how it's going. Slow, I think. Too damn slow.

Another conductor enters my compartment. White shirt, navy pants, cap on his head, black bag hanging from his shoulder. I hand him my ticket, he thanks me, inspects it carefully, runs a finger over it.

"To Šid?" he asks.

"To Šid," I reply.

He returns the ticket, wishes me a good trip, and says I can stop by the snack bar if I want. I thank him. I take my backpack down from the rack. Some coffee would do me good. The other passengers are napping in their compartments. The train lists gently, first to the left, then to the right. I can hear the rumbling of the radio coming from the snack bar. I enter, and a waiter with a dirty rag slung over his shoulder nods at me. Small tables in the shape of an ironing board line the perimeter. A stool is affixed to each side of the table. I order espresso.

"We don't have any," the waiter says. "Just Bosnian coffee."

"I'll take that," I reply, "and a mineral water."

There's an old man sitting there too. He's drinking rakija. A book and hat on the table in front of him. I sip the scalding coffee. Grounds stick to my tongue. We wobble gently. I stare out into the night. It obscures our path, as if ashamed. The locomotive squeals, the wheels sputter.

"In Tito's day it was much better," declares the old man.

The waiter exits carrying a tray with bottles of beer and cola. Having lost his interlocutor, the old man turns to me. He smiles weakly. "You're from Sarajevo?" Something about him seems familiar and close. I nod, and he picks up his hat and book, taking a seat next to me. His name is Jakov. He's from

Belgrade, where he's now returning after burying his sister yesterday in Sarajevo. His book is an old photo album, the directory and compass of his life. On the first page are black-and-white photographs of smiling people. Jakov leafs through it ever more slowly. "My child, I now have more people under the ground than above it." His parents and brother were killed at Jasenovac. His fingers slowly turn to pages with color photos. "That's Roza, my sister. We were the only two to survive that war." He takes a deep breath. Keeps leafing through the album. We arrive at pages without pictures. Instead there are obituaries. Roza's is the last among them. "And then war came again. Roza in Sarajevo. Me in Belgrade. Fate." Silently we look at the smiling Roza. The old man closes the funereal book, strokes its cover, and says, "So, everyone's in there. My Roza too. I'm the only one missing."

Locomotive 3

We enter Croatia at night and sit on the tracks. There's a clanging sound as the workers remove the locomotive of Republika Srpska. We pass through customs while waiting for them to attach the locomotive of the Republic of Croatia. Jakov and I sit in the dingy fluorescent light of the snack bar. He reminds me of my grandfather. I rarely talk about him, but tonight, on the old Olympic Express, I tell Grandpa's stories to this man named Jakov. He was another good man orphaned after the Second World War. From Kozara. His parents were killed in the village. The state raised him. Eventually he embraced Grandma's hometown as his own. Her family became his.

A third conductor enters. White shirt, navy pants, cap on his head, black bag hanging from his shoulder. I hand him my ticket, he thanks me, inspects it carefully, runs a finger over it.

"To Šid?" he asks.

"To Šid," I reply.

Jakov takes out his ticket. The conductor thanks us and moves on. I can't stop talking about my grandpa, who loved Tito almost as much as he loved us. When he was eight years old he was living in an orphanage in Ljubljana. It was a boarding school too. The children spent twenty-four hours a day with their teachers and caregivers. One day, Tito came for a visit. They were skinny kids with Young Pioneer caps on their shaved heads, and he was the top man, the leader. Tito sent all the teachers out of the room, crouched down, and asked, "Children, do you have balls to play with?" They trembled, silent. One little voice piped up from the last row. "Sort of, we make them from socks." "Do your teachers beat you?" asked Tito. Frightened, they didn't dare speak. Again that little voice rose and pronounced the name of one of the teachers. Tito nodded. At this, others were encouraged, and names poured forth like summer rain. Every time he'd tell me this story, my grandpa's voice would grow softer, gentler. He'd never fail to mention that he had also snitched on one of the teachers. The next day, the children woke to the rumble of a truck. They all ran to the windows. It was a sight to behold. The teachers were hauling huge baskets of balls from the truck. And it was only those teachers whose names hadn't been disclosed. The children never saw the violent and strict ones again.

Jakov won't let me pay for my coffee. He shakes my hand firmly and orders another rakija. I return to my compartment. Silence still presides over the train. The passengers' drowsy thoughts are knitted with the winter night like black strands in a ball of yarn. We pass through Tovarnik. Soon we'll be at another border.

Locomotive 4

The locomotive of the Republic of Croatia leaves us. The customs officers have done their work and now we wait to take on the locomotive of the Republic of Serbia. It's no more than twenty minutes now till the station in Šid. I'm nervous, a little panicky. I open the window and smoke. Fifteen fucking years. The drawn-out crunching sound of metal on metal. A fourth conductor enters. White shirt, navy pants, cap on his head, black bag hanging from his shoulder. I hand him my ticket, he thanks me, inspects it carefully, runs a finger over it.

"From Sarajevo?" he asks.

"From Sarajevo," I reply.

He raises his cap in a sign of greeting and leaves. I zip up my jacket and put on my hat. My backpack is ready. I hop around in place. My stomach tightens. My great aunt sends another message. It says that everyone's there, just waiting for me. We pull into the station. I feel uneasy.

The hobbled train departs. I watch it go. It's for the best that Grandpa's not here. He wasn't made for this world and this travel. For locomotives that can't cross their own borders.

Sneža and the Bačinci Dwarves

THIS IS A STORY about Sneža and the Bačinci Dwarves. Once upon a time, they lived in their village. Happy, playing in the mud.

I love that village near Šid where my grandmother and mother were born. Everyone there calls me Lejla, Sneža's baby girl. In the afternoon, when we've finished having lunch, I go for a walk. Grandmas and grandpas, and sometimes younger people too, sit on the benches in front of their little houses. Just yesterday I met Sneža's dwarves: Steva, Rade, Zvonko, Želja. They gathered outside of Rade's house, hopped in place, told jokes, smoked. Their hands calloused, their noses red. They smelled like milk. They wore wool caps, vests, and muddy boots. I greeted them. Their smiles were gentle and wistful.

They remember Sneža. How could they forget her, they insist. They reminisce about her, her muddy rubber boots, her childhood spent in the churchyard. They were an inseparable clan, until Sneža's mother took her away to the city. They grew up, and Sneža would come to Grandma Sofija's in the summer.

"Our Sneža would come. So beautiful, the fairest of them all," says Steva.

"A city girl. A Sarajka!" You could see Želja's breath.

"We were ragamuffins, bumpkins. Ashamed in our Sneža's presence. We didn't dare get too close. We'd gather in Rade's yard to peep through the fence," says Zvonko.

The others nod.

"She'd bring a typewriter," Steva mimics her fingers tapping the keys, "tap tap tap, all day long. Sometimes she'd come out in the yard. And laugh loudly."

"Lovely. City girl, the fairest of them all," repeats Steva.

"All her dresses were beautiful," calls out Rade.

They glance at each other. Their eyebrows furrow. They know everything about her death.

"Our Sneža left for the city. She got married there," continues Želja. "But here, life was once good for us here in the village. Children are children, after all. We were happy."

"Sneža had a daughter in the city. A daughter. You." Steva smiles.

They fall silent. I hop in place with them, me, Sneža's baby girl. We gaze down the village road.

Rade turns toward me. "What can I say, child. The city is your stepmother."

The Wizard

THE MOONLIGHT WAS shining. Georges canceled that night's appearance and sprinted down the Boulevard des Italiens. He arrived right on time at the Grand Café, trembling from the effort.

"Please," said Georges to Claude Antoine after the screening. "I beg you."

The proud sons of Lumière were buying their fame in the front room when old Claude Antoine agreed to a meeting with this strange fellow who was rumored to perform all sorts of magic. The old man shook his head and tapped his heel on the floor. Yes, indeed, he pitied the quixotic Georges.

"Sir, I cannot. There's no way!"

Georges eyes filled with tears. His Adam's apple contracted. He could barely breathe.

"Be reasonable. I have no intention of taking your money. No," the "o" rolled around his palate like a glass marble, "this is not for art's sake. This is for science! That gadget has no future."

He thought of the filmmaker. He stroked his gray beard. The same one that, it should be noted, Georges later donated to the scientists in his film.

The Parisian evenings were cold in December. Rejected and ashamed, Georges sat on the steps of his theater long into the night. Everyone had left hours before. They were dreaming in their beds. Just two dogs meandered up and down the boulevard, sniffing for food scraps. All the lights in the building were off. The nest of magic rested in its own cavernous dream. The moonlight was shining.

* * *

December, a holiday mood in my great aunt's village home, where my mother and grandmother were born. I arrived a few days ago, at the former nest of our family life. We sit at the table and eat. Auntie, Uncle, and I. The chicken is tender and juicy. The drumstick meat slides easily off the bone, I note while taking a bite. Auntie nods. The bakery's oven rules. I've never eaten a better baked potato. There's also homemade rakija on the table, and Auntie pours three small glasses for us. We're chewing, swallowing huge mouthfuls; Auntie puts the wings on my plate, and I can't help but recall aloud how my grandmother loved to gnaw on chicken wings.

"No one knew how to enjoy food as much as she did!" says Uncle.

We laugh. And then it's as if something has pricked him. He suddenly rises from his chair and bangs his fist on the table.

"Oh, for fuck's sake! I almost forgot!"

I look at him, confused. Keep chewing.

"Lelo," he says, drawing out the "o," "I have something for you, something you've never seen."

He quickly wipes his hands with a dish towel and goes into the other room. Auntie calls out in vain that he should finish his lunch first "like a normal person."

On the table sits an oval platter with little cakes. We sip rakija while water for coffee heats up on the stove. Uncle and I smoke; Auntie grabs the jar of coffee and opens the little kitchen window. I'm turning over a DVD in my hands. My great uncle, the baker, sometime photographer for the Grafosrem printing company in Šid, made a summer project of cleaning up the attic and organizing thousands of family photographs. Before the war, whenever Grandma, Grandpa, and I would come for a visit, it felt like we'd spend the entire ten days just looking at photos. I didn't know there were recordings too. Uncle tells me he had a Super 8, and with the same passion and dedication he'd filmed home movies of our everyday life. Working in the attic, he came across a recording from '74.

"You have to see it," he says.

He takes the DVD from my hands and sticks it in the player. Auntie asks me if I want some milk in my coffee and I shake my head no. The little film begins. In the frame appears the old house in Šid. A table in the living room. At the table are seated Grandma, Grandpa, Auntie, and a fourteen-year-old girl. Grandma and Auntie whip around in the direction of Uncle's camera, so quickly they disrupt the shot. I look at the girl, my long-dead mother. She sits in a chair, directly across from the camera. She is smiling. Her feet don't touch the ground. She dangles first one leg, then the other, in white knee socks. The family idyll, captured in a few minutes. The girl doesn't shrink from the camera. Her gaze is restless and intense. We watch each other, eye to eye. Me and Mama, who never existed in my memory. Her hair is thick and black. Straight bangs, and the rest flows to her shoulders. We watch each other. I'm a little hazy from the rakija. The magic spell moves across the screen, turning into my inebriated thoughts.

Auntie and Uncle are silent. I say I'm going to go stretch my legs. Colorful lights glint in the windows of the village houses.

The street is deserted. And then, on the other side, under a locust tree, I catch sight of him. He's walking in a circle, as if waiting for someone. I watch his steps, tentative and small, like I imagine everyone's to be when they're sleepy. He shuffled along just like that, I believe, in his bankrupt years, on the Boulevard des Italiens, outside his desolate nest of magic.

We meet again, the Wizard and I. The first time was in the damp winter screening room of the Kinoteka, when I saw *A Trip to the Moon*. And now, in the holiday night, in the village called Bačinci, in the street lined with locust trees. In a long woolen coat. He notices me, takes off his astral hat, bows his head in the manner of a great maestro. There's so much I want to tell him. But one thanks would be enough. I'm just about to speak when the front door to my great aunt's house opens. Light escapes from the vestibule. The Wizard, startled, leaps to the side, and I simply raise my hand. I watch him disappear down the street, fade into the distance, his steps light like raven feathers. I wave at him. Bye, Georges. Farewell, Méliès. May the moonlight keep you safe!

I drop my cigarette butt in the grass and crush it with my foot. I hurry back up the stairs. Through the open door I hear: "Come on, it's time for dinner."

Why Do Sparrows Die?

DURING THE RAINY season, when someone invokes the summer and the sea, I think of the sparrows.

Late summer '91. Dad and I are at a little resort that the post office keeps for its workers' use, ensconced in a cove halfway between the hotels Zenit and Sunce. There's Dad's colleague Samir, Samir's girlfriend Mira from Novi Sad, Rade, a veterinary student, and a teenage girl named Bilja, whose boobs the waiters stare at incessantly. We gather at the beach day and night, playing pool, dominoes, cards. Two days before our return home, Samir heads to Sarajevo in his new Yugo to pick up his brother and parents. This puts Mira in a state. She's afraid of the dark and the solitude of their hotel room. Dad lets me stay with her.

That summer night, while we joke around, while I try to speak her ekavian dialect and she, my ijekavian dialect, ominous clouds roll in. The Bura wind arrives around 10:00pm, in the middle of our rummy game. The clouds and waves begin to do battle. The wind blows away everything in its path. The hotel windows quiver. In the garden of the resort, the umbrellas split apart and the tables and chairs flip over. The waves crash against the rocks. Suddenly, lightning flashes like a giant neon sign. Mira screams, making the hair on my arms stand on end and my heart jump in my chest, but I quickly calm down. I console her.

The morning after the great battle of heaven and earth. The adults survey the damage, walking around in their track suits, inspecting the shoreline and the snapped trees. I look at the sparrows, flipped on their backs, their little legs pointed toward the sky. In the fallen leaves of a wounded tree lie dozens of them. Rade organizes a procession, with himself, the young veterinarian, at the front, and Bilja and me behind him. He lightly places each baby bird in his palm, brings its beak to his ear, and listens. A few are still alive. "Pneumonia," Rade pronounces. Then we return them to their deathbeds, because there's nothing we can do. The birds die slowly, in drawn-out cries.

Samir and Mira's love ended at the beginning of the war. I heard nothing more about Rade. They say Bilja fled with her family to Northern Europe.

I live near Grbavica Stadium. On my street there's a big row of plane trees, two birch trees, one weeping willow, and an enormous wild chestnut. Whenever storm clouds gather above the city at night, I lie in bed, wrap myself in the covers, and think of the birds. I carry these thoughts into sleep. All night I dream of getting out of bed, putting on my jacket and shoes, and slowly venturing out into the night.

In the abandoned street, the branches drip the last traces of the storm. I'm at the front of the procession, followed by darkness and wind. It's eerily quiet. I walk from tree to tree, lingering at each one, ducking under its broken branches. I pick up the sparrows, listen to their fear, their thin cries for life, then return them to the cold, wet leaves.

Das Ist Walter

"HEY, WHAT BRINGS you here?" they ask in unison as I approach the military base, out of breath.

"Nothing in particular." I inhale deeply, my hands gripping my knees. "What are all of you doing here?"

"We're from here," laughs Mrva.

"Well fuck it, so am I." I try to take in as much air as I can, while they chuckle at my discomfort.

"It's because you don't come here that often," says Belma, moving over to make room for me.

* * *

We're kids from Jajačka Street. It got its name from Jajce, the base where we hung out growing up. The base that was burned down, rebuilt, destroyed again, turned into a festering black wound from which slithered snakes half a meter long. But it also had its glory days. In a film we adored.

"I want to."

"No, no, I want to."

"No, me!"

"I'll say it: Das ist Walter!"

That's how we, the children of Jajačka Street, would fight over who would get to play the role in the final scene of the celebrated film *Valter brani Sarajevo*. We had everything we needed: the city's panorama below us, the base behind. Instead of a movie camera, ten little eyes watching while you recited those momentous words. Sometimes we'd have an even bigger audience. We'd show off our acting chops to a group of soldiers standing guard. They'd offer us their applause, sometimes chocolate too.

We loved the new recruits. We learned from them—more than from our science and social studies classes—how big and beautiful our homeland was. They'd often ask us to get them cigarettes, juice, or snacks from the corner store. They'd stick their fingers through the thick grating on the barracks windows to pass us their cash. We'd come running up to the gate to deliver the bags full of supplies. They'd leave us the change so we could buy chewing gum.

There were misunderstandings too. When we'd play picigen, we'd use the wall of the barracks as an imaginary goalpost. After we ignored their warnings, the soldiers we'd awakened would stick a hose through the window grates and spray us with water. We'd retaliate by sneaking fresh eggs from our houses and throwing them at the barracks. The soldiers would swear and threaten to have the officers court-martial us. Like mice in the presence of a cat, we'd scatter, biting our lips as we ran home terrified that some general was coming to arrest us.

*   *   *

The wall warms the backs of our adult bodies, reheating the memories in our tired minds. No one asks again why I'm here. The words pull us backward, to Walter, the soldiers, the shit we

LEJLA KALAMUJIĆ

got up to. We peer into the courtyard beyond the gates, where strange grass pokes out of cracks in the concrete. There's trash too, rust, dog shit, and so much emptiness it makes our skin crawl. Mrva, whose house sits right across the street from the base, says that nighttime is the worst. Dogs howl and bark, cats mate, and the wind roars, rattling the heavy iron grates, the creaky ancient doorframes. Such nothingness frightens the living. No one dares go inside, especially given the snakes. Today we're all afraid of the base.

* * *

Sometimes the soldiers, in search of a little entertainment, would rip a few tiles from the barracks roof and quietly, as we watched them breathlessly from down below, skate one by one along the loose gutter like giant raindrops. We worried that some officer, noticing their absence, would accuse them of deserting, and us of keeping their violations to ourselves.

Once we were truly terrified. I don't remember what time of year it was, but I know the weather was nice. Edo and I were on our way to Mejdan to buy something when we were startled by the sound of military boots coming from down the street. This alone wouldn't have made us look back—we were used to the soldiers going out for exercises—so we didn't see the strange and serious faces of the soldiers marching past. They were in full uniform, with helmets on their heads. We stopped, took in the sight of them, and quick as a flash ran back the way we'd come, screaming at the top of our lungs: "The Germans! The Germans are attacking us!"

A commotion rose up. It made some of the grandmas ill to hear our screaming. They thought a child had been harmed. All day a state of emergency reigned over Jajačka Street. The whole neighborhood poured into Edina's garden. When asked where we'd gotten the idea of a German attack, we tried in vain to explain that in all the Partisan films the Germans wore helmets, and our soldiers, only hats. Edo was forbidden from watching TV for a month, and in the ensuing days the adults monitored our playtime for any new conspiracies.

But we didn't know about conspiracies for a long time.

No one noticed the soldiers' departure, except for two eventual tanks, once the war had already begun.

Then the base was a shelter, then once more a base.

No one remembers when it became deserted again.

When did it fall to ruin?

When did it begin to inspire such great fear?

When did we grow up?

Stop hanging out?

Meet again?

* * *

Our bodies merge on that spring day while we sit outside our base. We gaze at the city below us in silence. The sun's glare obscures everything. We can't see the rooftops, the buildings, the people in the streets. Just like we never noticed when Walter left.

LEJLA KALAMUJIĆ

Back Among the Stars

THEY SAY THAT Bare is one of the biggest urban cemeteries in Europe. On thirty-three hectares lie 60,000 graves. One-seventh of the population in Sarajevo today. Nevertheless, a discord exists, a deep abyss between the living and the dead. An abyss twenty years deep, bridged by the decision that, after a long absence, I'll go up, into the high terrain of Bare. They built atheist plots there in a project organized by Smiljan Klaić, a famous twentieth century Croatian urbanist and landscape architect. Naida comes with me. For years I've promised to take her to my mother's grave, atheist grave #13, which affords a lovely view of the landmark TV transmitter on the hill known as Hum. They say, I brag to Naida, that Bare is one of the most interesting and beautiful eternal resting places in this part of the world. A hot spring day, like the air we quickly inhale as we climb. I'm carrying a tote bag with watering cans and a spade. I foisted a broom and two seedlings on Naida. The sun's rays connect the blocks of black and white marble to the sky. The soil on the road, dry as bone, crumbles under our feet. I'm trying to answer all of Naida's questions.

* * *

Saturday, during the summer holiday from daycare. I'm six years old. Grandma and Grandpa quietly sip coffee at the dining room table. I play on the floor, pushing a plastic jeep and making engine sounds. Grandma looks at me, then turns her head away. She looks at me again. She asks whether I'd like to go visit Mama. Grandma never uttered the word "grave." My lips grow numb from vrooming.

* * *

The ascent grows steeper, and we stop more often. Not a person in sight. On the gravestones of those long dead are scattered a few plastic flowers or the stumps of old candles.

* * *

Grandpa's large tears fall onto the white marble. They scatter into tiny droplets and disappear down the cracks of the gravestone. Grandma is busy. She arranges bouquets of fresh flowers in various vases, and takes the broom, bucket, and rags from her bag. She doles out our assignments, and the cleaning begins: we pull up the weeds, sweep the paths, scrub the headstone with Arf cleaner, rinse it over and over, and finally wipe everything dry. This was how my first outing to Mama's grave looked.

* * *

"It was like you were all at a work action," says Naida, laughing.
    "What can I say. For atheists, memories are a metaphysical category."

LEJLA KALAMUJIĆ

We go up to Bare every Saturday. Usually in the afternoon. We go to work, not to mourn. We plant flowers: petunias, violets, bluebells. It's our little Saturday ritual. Except on the coldest winter days. By November, Grandma and Grandpa have bought a thick nylon tarp they use to wrap up and tuck in the headstone, so the cold air won't damage it. Next to Vratnik and Grbavica, I know Bare best. I know the names, and often the causes of death, of those buried along the path leading from the gates to my mother's grave.

* * *

We pass by the halved marble apple, under which lies the Sarajevan musician Dražen Ričl. He was the first lead singer of the beloved 1980s rock band Crvena Jabuka. His is the most visited grave in all of Bare, I tell Naida. On the anniversary of his death, October 1, dozens of young people gather around the apple. They bring guitars and sing softly. As we get closer to it, the apple appears to have diminished in size. The world is somehow more spacious in my memories.

We climb to the top of the path where Plot A13 begins. I ask Naida to wait while I linger at the grave of a mother and her two children. A son and daughter, killed in a car accident in '84. On the headstone are engraved the name of the husband and father, and his date of birth with a hyphen. There's still no death date, I call out to Naida. I remember him well. Whenever we'd visit during my childhood, he would be there. He wore a gray, ankle-length coat and a round hat. He would huddle on the bench, smoking a cigar and staring into their carved faces. Grandma and Grandpa said he came every day after work, in summer and winter, rain or shine. He'd always stay there till night fell. I'd presumed that death had found him elsewhere, as it had Grandma and Grandpa.

Naida hurries me along. To appease her, I say we're very close and point toward my mother's grave. There are several other graves just like it. In the early '80s it was common to make headstones in the shape of three leaves for the graves of younger people.

"It'll be faster if we cut through," I say, pulling her by the hand.

We can hear dogs barking on Hum. We stand near the gravesite. Naida looks at me questioningly. I begin to list our tasks: "The small vase is leaking again, the large one cracked. It needs to be glued. The marble is damaged. See these dark veins running through it? They need to be buffed out." The tiles crunch beneath my feet. "They're broken, need to be replaced." I run my hand across the heart-shaped engraving where we planted flowers. Now only weeds bloom there.

Naida sits on the bench at the foot of the grave and reads aloud: "Snežana Kalamujić, née Ignjatović, 1960-1982."

I just stand there. Like Camus's *First Man*.

* * *

Summer of 2000. The reading room in the university library is full of students. Heat pours through the window. I read Camus, even though I should be studying for an exam. I'd rather read about the man who was only a year old when his father died in the Battle of the Marne. About the man who forty years later stood at the grave of his father, who'd been half his age.

* * *

LEJLA KALAMUJIĆ

That's me today. A thirty-year-old child at the grave of a twenty-two-year-old mother. I stand there, at an age she never reached. And everything somehow seems smaller and insufficient. The whole plot seems to have shrunk. Like a dress washed in too-hot water. We fall silent.

"Did you really wrap the headstone in plastic?" Naida asks.

I nod. We burst out laughing. Our voices reverberate on the hot stones.

Time passes. I remind Naida that we need to pull up the weeds before we leave. On my mother's plot, and on the two adjacent ones. She looks at me strangely.

"Right next to Mama, Tibor is buried," I explain. "He was twenty when he drowned. His father, who couldn't swim, watched from the shore as he sputtered in the waves. Next to Tibor is Ado. A three-year-old boy. Both of their parents left Sarajevo a long time ago, so when we'd come, we'd clean their graves too."

Naida just shakes her head and weeds.

It's getting cooler. I sweep the path. Every now and then I stop to gaze at the stars etched into the headstones. Some were in bronze, like Mama's, and others were in red, like the old flag. But now the color has faded. Their radiance has been tarnished by mold. We gather up everything. I put the flowerpots, spade, and broom back in my bag. I pull a pack of Drinas and a lighter from my pocket. I light one, take two drags to get it going, and then crush it into the ground, into the heart we've just cleaned of weeds.

The sun raises its anchor, leaving the cemetery to the onset of evening. In the silence resounds the thumping of our footsteps. Slowly we descend toward the chapels. Naida takes out the piece of paper where she wrote down the bus schedule. We pass by a hunched old man in a hat. As if someone's punched me in the stomach, I come to a halt and grab Naida's elbow.

"What's wrong?"

"That's him!"

I run back uphill, trying to reach him. Naida yells to me. I wave at him.

"Excuse me, excuse me!"

The old man stops and turns. I finally catch up, gasping. He looks at me questioningly.

"May I help you?"

"It's just that I'm . . ."

"Yes?"

"You see, I remember you. My mother was buried here in '82." I point to her grave. "Before the war I came here all the time with my grandmother and grandfather. You were always here. We would greet each other."

The old man contemplates this for a moment. He looks in the direction of my mother's plot.

"Yes, yes." He nods.

I smile as much as I can. I'm as happy as if I'd met my closest kin.

"And them?" he asks.

"Who?"

"Your grandparents."

"Dead."

"Are they here too?" He waves his hand in the air as if caressing the graves.

"No. They're not here."

He doesn't say anything. He looks down, knowing it's better not to inquire further. We say goodbye. He slowly proceeds to his plot. I watch how he weaves through the graves. How he sits on the same bench and lights his cigar. I don't know anyone who's waited so long for death to come. I look at the atheist plot behind me. I want to make sure one last time that everything is in its place.

LEJLA KALAMUJIĆ

* * *

Naida is fidgeting from impatience. She waves at me to hurry up, we're going to be late for the bus. I make my way to her. It's time to go. It's time.

LEJLA KALAMUJIĆ is an award-winning queer writer from Bosnia and Herzegovina. *Call Me Esteban* received the Edo Budiša literary award in 2016 and it was the Bosnian-Herzegovinian nominee for the European Union Prize for Literature in the same year.

JENNIFER ZOBLE translates Bosnian/Croatian/Serbian- and Spanish-language literature. Her translation of *Mars* by Asja Bakić (Feminist Press, 2019) was selected by *Publishers Weekly* for the fiction list in its "Best Books 2019" issue. She contributed to the anthology *Belgrade Noir* (Akashic Books, 2020), and her work has been published in *McSweeney's, Lit Hub, Words Without Borders, Washington Square, The Iowa Review*, and *The Baffler*, among others. She's on the Liberal Studies faculty at NYU, where she teaches writing and translation.